HAVERHILL
PUBLIC LIBRARY

This item was purchased with
funds from private donors to
maintain the collection of the
Haverhill Public Library.

D1416344

For Trisha, for everything

Copyright © 2011 by Stephen Shaskan.
All rights reserved. No part of this book may be reproduced in
any form without written permission from the publisher.

Library of Congress Cataloging-in-Publication Data available.

ISBN 978-0-8118-7896-8

Book design by Aimee Gauthier.
Typeset in Chaloops.
The illustrations in this book were rendered digitally.

Manufactured by Toppan Leefung, Da Ling Shan Town, Dongguan, China, in January 2012.

10 9 8 7 6 5 4 3 2

This product conforms to CPSIA 2008.

Chronicle Books LLC
680 Second Street, San Francisco, California 94107

www.chroniclekids.com

MIX
Paper from
responsible sources
FSC® C104723
FSC
www.fsc.org

A DOG Is a DOG

By Stephen Shaskan

chronicle books · san francisco

A dog is a dog,

whether it's naughty . . .

. . . or nice.

Whether it suns on the beach,

or glides on the ice.

A dog is a dog, if it's skinny or fat.

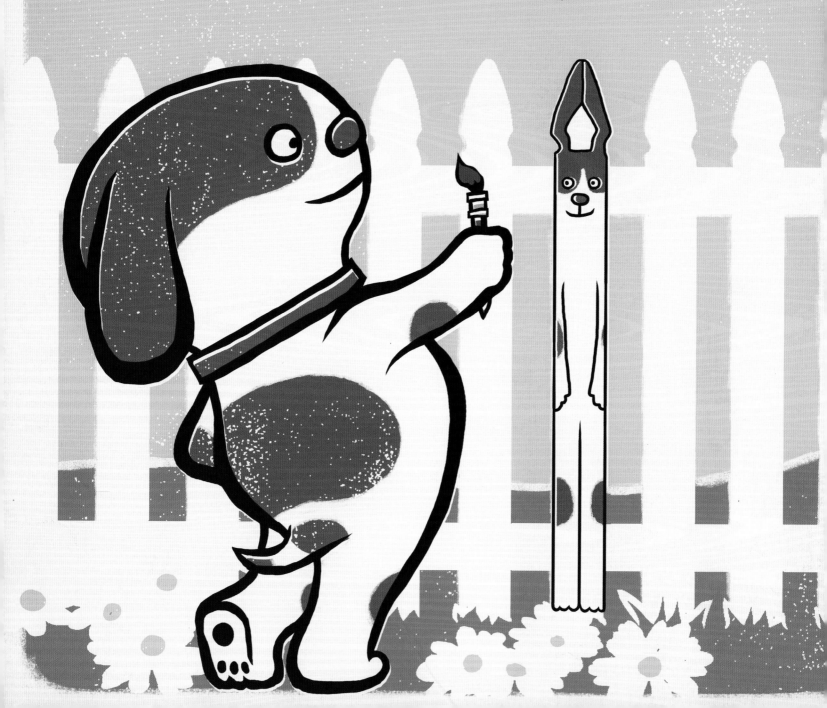

A dog is a dog, unless it's a . . .

CAT!

A cat is a cat, whether it hisses . . .

. . . or purrs.

Whether it's hairless and cold,

or wrapped up in furs.

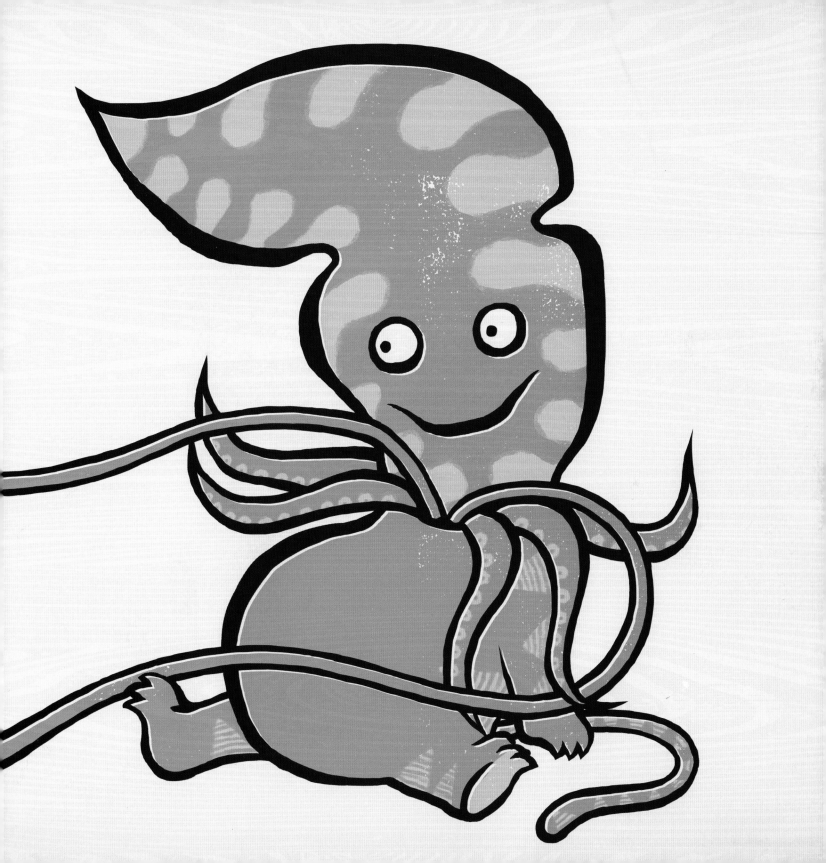

A squid is a squid, whether it's fast . . .

. . . or it's slow.

Whether it swims up on top . . .

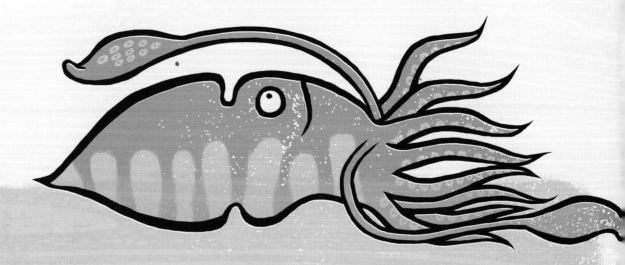

. . . or swims down below.

A squid is a squid,
when it's stuck . . .

A moose is a moose,
whether it's large . . .

. . . or it's small.

A moose is a moose, in the clear . . .

DOG.